Indian Nocturne

Also by Antonio Tabucchi

LETTER FROM CASABLANCA
(Translated by Janice M. Thresher)

LITTLE MISUNDERSTANDINGS OF NO IMPORTANCE
(Translated by Frances Frenaye)

Indian Nocturne

A NOVELLA BY ANTONIO TABUCCHI

TRANSLATED BY TIM PARKS

A NEW DIRECTIONS BOOK

1984 © Sellerio editore
Translation copyright © 1988 Chatto & Windus Ltd.

Published by arrangement with Chatto & Windus Ltd., London
Manufactured in the United States of America
New Directions Books are printed on acid-free paper
This translation of Notturno indiano first published
clothbound in the United States and as New Directions
Paperbook 666 in 1989

Library of Congress Cataloging-in-Publication Data

Tabucchi, Antonio, 1943–
    Indian nocturne.
    (A New Directions Book)
    Translation of: Notturno indiano.
    I. Title.
PQ4880.A24N6813   1989   853'.914   88–5169

ISBN-13: 978-0-8112-1080-5
ISBN-10: 0-8112-1080-4

New Directions Books are published for James Laughlin
by New Directions Publishing Corporation,
80 Eighth Avenue, New York 10011

THIRD PRINTING

Those who sleep badly seem to a greater or lesser degree guilty: what do they do? They make the night present.

Maurice Blanchot

Author's Note

As well as being an insomnia, this book is also a journey. The insomnia belongs to the writer of the book, the journey to the person who did the travelling. All the same, given that I too happen to have been through the same places as the protagonist of this story, it seemed fitting to supply a brief index of the various locations. I don't really know whether this idea was prompted by the illusion that a topographical inventory, with the force that the real possesses, might throw some light on this Nocturne in which a Shadow is sought; or whether by the irrational conjecture that some lover of unlikely itineraries might one day use it as a guide.

A.T.

Index of the Places in this book

Indian Nocturne

I

The taxi driver wore a hairnet and had a pointed beard and a short ponytail tied with a white ribbon. I thought he might be a Sikh, since my guidebook described them as looking exactly like that. My guidebook was called *India, a Travel Survival Kit*; I'd bought it in London, more out of curiosity than anything else, since the information it offered about India was fairly bizarre and at first glance superfluous. Only later was I to realize how useful it could be.

The Sikh was driving too fast for my liking and hitting his horn ferociously. I had the impression he was deliberately going as close to the pedestrians as he could, and with an indefinable smile on his face that I didn't like. On his right hand he wore a black glove, and I didn't like that either. When he turned into Marine Drive he seemed to calm down and quietly took his place in one of the lines of traffic on the side nearest the sea. With his gloved hand he pointed to the palm trees along the seafront and the curve of the bay. "That's Trobay," he said, "and opposite us is Elephant Island, only you can't see it. I'm sure you'll be wanting to go there, the ferries leave every hour from the Gateway of India."

I asked him why he was going down Marine Drive. I didn't know Bombay, but I was trying to follow our route on a map on my knees. My reference points were Malabar Hill and the Chor, the Thieves' Market. My hotel was somewhere between those two points, and there was no need to go along Marine Drive to get to it. We were driving in the opposite direction.

"The hotel you mentioned is in a very poor district," he said affably, "and the goods are very poor quality. Tourists on their first trip to Bombay often end up in the wrong sort of place. I'm taking you to a hotel suitable for a gentleman like yourself." He spat out of the window and winked. "Where the goods are top quality." He gave me a sleazy smile of great complicity, and this I liked even less.

"Stop here," I said, "at once."

He turned round and looked at me with a servile expression. "But I can't stop here," he said, "there's the traffic."

"Then I'll get out anyway," I said, opening the door and holding it tight.

He braked sharply and began a litany in a language that must have been Marathi. He looked furious and I don't suppose the words he was hissing through his teeth were particularly polite, but I didn't take any notice. I had only the one small suitcase which I had kept beside me, so there wasn't even any need for him to get out and get me my luggage. I left him a hundred-rupee note and climbed out onto the vast pavement of Marine Drive. On the beach there was a religious festival, or fair, one or the other, with a big crowd milling in front of something I couldn't make out. Along

4

the seafront there were bums stretched out on the parapet, children selling knick-knacks, beggars. There was also a line of motorized rickshaws; I jumped into a sort of yellow cubicle hitched up to a moped and shouted the name of the street my hotel was on to the small driver. He stamped on the starter pedal and set off at full speed, slipping into the traffic.

Cage District was much worse than I had imagined. I'd seen it in the photographs of a famous photographer and thought I was prepared for human misery, but photographs enclose the visible in a rectangle. The visible without a frame is always something else. And then here the visible had too strong a smell. Or rather smells, a lot of smells.

It was dusk when we entered the district, and in the time it took to go down a street, quite suddenly, as happens in the tropics, night fell. Many of the buildings in Cage District are made of wood and matting. Prostitutes wait in shacks made of ill-fitting boards, their heads sticking out of holes. Some of those shacks were not much larger than sentry-boxes. And then there were hovels and tents of rags, little shops perhaps or other kinds of business, lit by paraffin lamps, with small clusters of people in front. But the Hotel Khajuraho had a small illuminated sign and opened almost on the corner of a street with brick buildings, and the lobby, if you could call it that, was merely ambiguous without being sordid. It was a small dark room with a high counter like the bars in English pubs; at each end of the counter were two lamps with red shades and behind it was an old woman. She wore a gaudy sari and her nails were painted blue; by the looks of her she could have been European, although on her forehead she wore one of the many marks that Indian women do wear. I showed her my passport and told her I'd booked by telegram. She nodded and began to copy from my passport making a great show of how careful she was being, then she turned the paper round for me to sign.

"With bathroom or without?" she asked, and told me the price.

I took a room with a bathroom. I had the impression she spoke with a slight American accent, but I didn't go into it.

She told me the room number and handed me the key. The keyring was made of transparent plastic with a design inside of the kind you might expect in a hotel like this. "Do you want dinner?" she asked. She looked at me suspiciously. I got the message that the place was not usually used by Westerners. Naturally she was wondering what I was doing there with hardly any luggage after having cabled from the airport.

I said yes. Not that eating in the hotel was a particularly pleasant prospect, but I was very hungry and it didn't seem a good idea to start wandering around the area at this hour.

"The dining room closes at eight," she said. "After eight it's room-service only."

I said I'd prefer to eat downstairs; she led me to a curtain on the other side of the lobby and I went through into a small vaulted room with darkly painted walls and low tables. The tables were almost all free and the light very dim. The menu promised an infinite variety of dishes, but on asking the waiter I discovered that just that particular evening they were all off. Except for number fifteen. I dined swiftly on rice and fish, drank a warm beer and went back to the lobby. The woman was still on her seat and seemed intent on arranging some coloured stones on a kind of mirror. On the small sofa in the corner, near the main door, sat two very dark young men, wearing Western style dress, with flared trousers. They acted as if they hadn't noticed me, but I immediately sensed a certain unease. I went up to the counter and waited for her to speak first. Which she did. She said some numbers in a neutral detached voice; I didn't get exactly what she meant and asked her to repeat. It was a price list. The only figures I understood were the first and the last; from thirteen to fifteen years old, three hundred rupees, over fifty, five rupees.

"The women are in the lounge on the first floor," she finished.

I took the letter from my pocket and showed her the signature. I had memorized the name, but I preferred to let her see it written so that there would be no misunderstanding. "Vimala Sar," I said. "I want a girl called Vimala Sar."

She threw a quick glance at the two young men sitting on the sofa. "Vimala Sar doesn't work here any more," she said. "She's left."

"Where did she go?" I asked.

"I don't know," she said, "but we have prettier girls than her."

The situation didn't look promising. Out of the corner of my eye I thought I saw the two youths shift a little, but maybe it was just an impression.

"Find her for me," I said quickly. "I'll wait in my room." Fortunately I had two twenty-dollar bills in my pocket. I laid them among the coloured stones and picked up my suitcase. As I was climbing the stairs I had a small inspiration dictated by fear. "My embassy knows I'm here," I said in a loud voice.

The room looked clean. It was painted a light green colour and on the walls were prints showing what looked like the erotic sculptures of Khajuraho, but I didn't particularly feel like checking. The bed was very low with a tattered armchair next to it and a small mountain of coloured cushions. On the bedside table were various objects whose purpose could not be misunderstood. I undressed and found some clean underwear. The bathroom was a painted cubbyhole with a poster on the door showing a blonde straddling a bottle of Coca Cola. The poster was yellow with age and smutted by insects, the blonde wore her hair *à la* Marilyn Monroe, fifties style, which made her look even more incongruous. The shower had no shower head, it was simply a pipe sticking out of the wall with a jet of water that gushed out at head height. Still, washing seemed the most voluptuous thing in the world: I had an eight-hour flight behind me, plus three hours in the airport and then the ride across Bombay.

I don't know how long I slept. Perhaps two hours, perhaps longer. When the knocking on the door woke me I automatically went to answer, not even realizing where I was at first. The girl entered with a rustle of clothes. She was small and wore a pretty sari. She was sweating and her make-up was running at the corners of her eyes. She said: "Good evening, sir, I am Vimala Sar." She stood in the middle of the room, her eyes down and arms at her sides, as if I was supposed to inspect her.

"I'm a friend of Xavier's," I said.

She lifted her eyes and I saw the total amazement on her face. I had set up her letter on the bedside table. She looked at it and began to cry.

"How come he ended up in this place?" I asked. "What was he doing here? Where is he now?"

She began to sob softly and I realized I'd asked too many questions.

"Take it easy," I said.

"When he found out I'd written to you he was very angry," she said.

"And why did you write to me?"

"Because I found your address in Xavier's diary," she said. "I knew you were good friends, once."

"Why was he angry?"

She put a hand to her mouth as if to stop herself crying. "He'd got to be very hard on me those last months," she said. "He was ill."

"But what was he doing?"

"He was doing business," she said. "I don't know, he didn't tell me anything, he'd stopped being nice to me."

"What kind of business?"

"I don't know," she repeated, "he didn't tell me anything. Sometimes he wouldn't say anything for days and days, then all of a sudden he'd get restless and flare up in a furious rage."

"When did he arrive here?"

"Last year," she said. "He came from Goa. He was doing business with them, then he fell ill."

"Them who?"

"The people in Goa," she said, "in Goa, I don't know." She sat on the armchair near the bed; she wasn't

9

crying now, she seemed calmer. "Get something to drink," she said. "There are drinks in the cabinet. A bottle costs fifty rupees."

I went to the cabinet and took a small bottle full of an orange liquid, a tangerine liqueur. "But who were the people in Goa?" I insisted. "Don't you remember the name, anything?"

She shook her head and began to cry again. "The people in Goa," she said, "in Goa, I don't know. He was ill," she repeated.

She paused and let out a long sigh. "Sometimes it seemed he didn't care about anything," she said, "not even me. The only thing that interested him at all were the letters from Madras, but then the next day he would be the same as before."

"What letters?"

"The letters from Madras," she said ingenuously, as if this were information enough.

"But who from?" I pressed her. "Who wrote to him?"

"I don't know," she said, "a society, I don't remember, he never let me read them."

"And he answered?"

Vimala sat there thinking. "Yes, he used to answer, I think he did, he spent hours and hours writing."

"Please," I said, "try to make an effort. What was this society?"

I don't know," she said, "it was a scholarly society I think, I don't know, sir." She paused again and then said: "He was a good man, he meant well. It was his nature. He had a sad destiny."

Her hands were clasped together, her fingers long and beautiful. Then she looked at me with an expression of relief, as if something had come back to her. "The Theosophical Society," she said. And for the first time she smiled.

"Listen," I said, "tell me everything, take your time, everything you remember, everything you can tell me."

I poured her another glass of the liqueur. She drank and began to tell. It was a long, rambling story, full of details. She talked about their affair, about the streets of Bombay, the holiday trips to Bassein and Elephanta. And then about afternoons at the Victoria Gardens, stretched out on the grass, about swimming at Chowpatty Beach under the first rains of the monsoon. I heard how Xavier had learnt to laugh and what he laughed about; and how much he liked the sunsets over the Arabian Sea when they walked along the seafront at dusk. It was a story she had carefully purged of any ugliness or misery. It was a love story.

"Xavier had written a great deal," she said, "then one day he burnt everything. Here in this hotel, he got a copper basin and burnt everything."

"Why?" I asked.

"He was ill," she said. "It was his nature. He had a sad destiny."

By the time Vimala left the night must have been over. I didn't look at my watch. I drew the curtains across the window and lay on the bed. Before falling asleep I heard a distant cry. Perhaps it was a prayer, or an invocation to the new day that was dawning.

II

"What was his name?"

"His name was Xavier," I answered.

"Like the missionary?" he asked. And then he said: "It's not an English name, that's for sure, is it?"

"No," I said, "it's Portuguese. But he didn't come as a missionary; he's a Portuguese who lost his way in India."

The doctor nodded his head in agreement. He had a gleaming hairpiece that shifted like a rubber skullcap every time he moved his head. "A lot of people lose their way in India," he said, "it's a country specially made for that."

I said: "Right." And then I looked at him and he looked at me without a trace of concern on his face, as if he were there by chance and everything else were where it was by chance, because that was how it had to be.

"Do you know his surname as well?" he asked, "It can be helpful sometimes."

"Janata Pinto," I said. "He had some distant connections with India, I think one of his ancestors was from Goa, or at least so he said."

The doctor made a gesture as if to say, that's enough, but that wasn't what he meant of course.

12

"There must be some records," I said, "or I hope there are."

He smiled with an unhappy, guilty look. He had very white teeth with a gap in the upper set. "Records . . ." he muttered. Suddenly his expression became hard and tense. He looked at me severely, almost contemptuously. "This hospital is in Bombay," he said abruptly, "you can forget your European notions, they are an arrogant luxury."

I said nothing and he too sat there silent. From his shirt pocket he pulled out a straw cigarette case and took a cigarette. Behind his table, on the wall, was a big clock. It said seven o'clock, it had stopped. I looked at it and he understood what I was thinking. "It stopped a long time ago," he said, "anyhow, it's midnight."

"I know," I said, "I've been waiting for you since eight, the day-doctor told me you were the only one who might be able to help me, he says you have a good memory."

He smiled again, his sad, guilty smile, and I realized that once again I'd slipped up, that it was not a gift to have a good memory in a place like this.

"He was a friend of yours?"

"In a way," I said, "once."

"When was he admitted?"

"Almost a year ago, I think, at the end of the monsoon."

"A year is a long time," he said. And then went on: "The monsoon is the worst season, so many people come in."

"I can imagine," I answered.

He put his head in his hands, as if he were thinking, or

as if he were very tired. "You can't imagine," he said. "Do you have a photograph of him?"

It was a simple, practical question, but I hesitated over the answer, for I too felt the weight of memory, and at the same time I sensed its inadequacy. What does one remember of a face in the end? No, I didn't have a photograph, I only had my memory: and my memory was mine alone, it wasn't describable, it was the look I remembered on Xavier's face. I made an effort and said: "He's the same height as I am, thin, with straight hair; he's about my age; sometimes he has an expression like yours, Doctor, because if he smiles he looks sad."

"It's not a very exact description," he said, "still, it makes no difference, I don't remember any Janata Pinto, at least not for the moment."

We were in a very grey, bare room. On the far wall was a large concrete sink, like the kind used for washing clothes. It was full of sheets of paper. Next to the sink was a long rough table and that too was laden with paper. The doctor got up and went to the far end of the room. He seemed to have a limp. He began to rummage through the papers on the table. From where I was I had the impression that they were pages from exercise books and pieces of brown wrapping paper.

"My records," he said, "each one is a name."

I stayed where I was in my seat facing his small work table, looking at the few objects he'd put there. There was a small glass ball with a model of Tower Bridge and a framed photograph showing a house that looked like a Swiss chalet. It struck me as absurd. At a window of the chalet you could see a female face, but the photograph was faded and blurred.

"He isn't an addict, is he?" he asked me from the other end of the room. "We don't admit addicts."

I didn't say anything and shook my head. "Not that I know of," I said then. "I don't think so, I'm not sure."

"But how do you know he came to the hospital, are you sure?"

"A prostitute at the Khajuraho hotel told me. That was where he was staying, last year."

"And you," he asked, "are you staying there too?"

"I slept there last night, but I'll leave tomorrow. I try not to stay more than a night in the same hotel, whenever possible."

"Why?" he asked, suspicious. He held an armful of papers and looked at me over his glasses.

"Just because," I said. "I like to change every night, I've only got this one small suitcase."

"And have you already decided for tomorrow?"

"Not yet," I said. "I think I'd like a very comfortable hotel, maybe a luxury one."

"You could go to the Taj Mahal," he said, "it's the most sumptuous hotel in the whole of Asia."

"Perhaps that's not a bad idea," I answered.

He plunged his arms into the sink amongst the pieces of paper. "So many people," he said. He had sat down on the rim of the basin and was cleaning his glasses. He rubbed his eyes with a handkerchief as if they were tired or irritated. "Dust," he said.

"The paper?" I said.

He lowered his eyes and turned away from me. "The paper," he said, "the people."

From the distance came a dark boom of iron, as though a bin were rolling down the stairs.

"Anyway, he's not there," he said, letting all the papers drop. "I don't think it's worth looking for him amongst these names."

Instinctively I got up. The moment had come for me to leave, I thought, that was what he was saying, that I should go. But he didn't seem to notice and went to a metal cabinet that once upon a time must have been painted white. He rummaged inside and took out some drugs which he hastily slipped into the pockets of his gown. I had the impression he was picking them up at random almost, without choosing them. "If he's still here, the only way to find him is to go and look for him," he said. "I have to do my round, if you want you can come along." He headed for the door and opened it. "I'll be doing a longer round than usual tonight, but perhaps you won't find it convenient to come with me."

I got up and followed him. "It's convenient," I said. "Can I bring my case with me?"

The door opened onto a hallway, a hexagonal space with a corridor leading off on every side. It was cluttered with cloths, bags and grey sheets. Some had purple or brown stains. We turned into the first corridor on our right; above the entrance was a plaque written in Hindu; some of the letters had fallen off leaving lighter outlines between the red letters.

"Don't touch anything," he said, "and don't go near the patients. You Europeans are very delicate."

The corridor was very long and was painted a melancholy light blue. The floor was black with cockroaches which burst under our shoes, though we were doing our best not to tread on them. "We kill them off," said the doctor, "but after a month they're back.

The walls are impregnated with larvae, you'd have to knock down the hospital."

The corridor ended in another hallway identical to the first, but narrow and light-less, closed off with a curtain.

"What did Mr Janata Pinto do?" he asked, pushing aside the curtain.

I thought of saying: "Simultaneous interpreter," which was what I should have said perhaps. Instead I said: "He wrote stories."

"Ah," he said. "Be careful, there's a step here. What were they about?"

"Oh," I said, "I wouldn't know how to explain really. I suppose you could say they were about things that didn't work out, about mistakes; for example, one was about a man who spends his life dreaming about making a trip, and when one day he's finally able to make it, that very day he realizes that he doesn't want to go any more."

"But he did set out on his trip," said the doctor.

"So it seems," I said. "Yes, he did."

The doctor let the curtains fall behind us. "There are about a hundred people in here," he said, "I'm afraid you won't find it a pleasant sight, they are the ones who have been here for some time. Your friend could be among them, although I think it's unlikely."

I followed him and we went into the largest room I have ever seen. It was as big as a hangar, almost, and along the walls and down three central rows were the beds, or rather mattresses. A few dim lamps hung from the ceiling, and I stopped a moment, because the smell was very strong. Crouching near the door were two men dressed in the barest rags who moved off as we came in.

"They are untouchables," said the doctor. "They look after the patients' bodily needs, no one else will do the job. India's like that."

In the first bed was an old man. He was completely naked and very thin. He looked dead, but kept his eyes wide open and looked at us without any trace of expression. He had an enormous penis curled up on his abdomen. The doctor went to him and touched his forehead. I thought he slipped a pill into his mouth, but I couldn't be sure because I was standing at the foot of the mattress. "He's a *sādhu*," said the doctor. "His genital organs are consecrated to God; once he was worshipped by infertile women, but he has never procreated in his life."

Then he moved on and I followed him. He stopped at every bed, while I hung back a short distance away looking at the patient's face. With some patients he stayed a while longer, murmuring a few words, distributing drugs. With others he stopped only a moment to touch their foreheads. The walls were stained red from the spittings of chewed betel and the heat was suffocating. Or perhaps it was the overpoweringly strong smell that gave this sensation of suffocation. In any case, the fans on the ceiling weren't working. Then the doctor turned back and I followed him in silence.

"He's not here," I said. "He's not one of these."

He pushed aside the curtain to the hall again with the same politeness as before, letting me lead the way.

"The heat is unbearable," I said, "and the fans aren't working. It's incredible."

"The voltage is very low at night in Bombay," he answered.

"And yet you have a nuclear reactor at Trobay, I saw the cooling tower from the front."

He smiled very weakly. "Almost all the energy goes to the factories, then to the luxury hotels and the Marine Drive area; here we have to make do." He set off along the corridor taking the opposite direction to the one we'd come from. "India's like that," he finished.

"Did you study here?" I asked.

He stopped to look at me and I had the impression that a flicker of nostalgia lit his eyes. "I studied in London," he said, "and then I did my specialization in Zürich." He brought out his straw cigarette case and took a cigarette. "An absurd specialization for India. I'm a cardiologist, but no one here has heart problems; only you people in Europe die of heart attacks."

"What do people die of here?" I asked.

"Of everything that has nothing to do with the heart. Syphilis, tuberculosis, leprosy, typhoid, septicaemia, cholera, meningitis, pellagra, diphtheria and other things. But I enjoyed studying the heart, I enjoyed finding out about that muscle that controls our lives, like this." He made a gesture, opening and closing his fist. "Perhaps I thought I would discover something inside it."

The corridor opened on to a small covered courtyard in front of a low brick building.

"Do you believe in God?" I asked.

"No," he said, "I'm an atheist. Being an atheist is the worst possible curse, in India."

We crossed the courtyard and stopped in front of the other building.

"The terminal cases are in here," he said, "there's just a chance your friend is one of them."

19

"What are they suffering from?" I asked.

"Everything you can possibly imagine," he said, "but perhaps it would be better if you went now."

"I think so too," I said.

"I'll show you out," he said.

"No, don't bother, please, perhaps I can get out through that door in the entrance gate. I think we're by the road here."

"My name's Ganesh," he said, "after the merry God with the elephant's face."

I told him my name too before setting off. The gate was only a moment away beyond a hedge of jasmin. It was open. When I turned to look back at him he spoke again. "If I find him, should I say something?"

"No thanks," I said, "don't say anything."

He raised his hairpiece as if it were a hat and made a slight bow. I went out into the street. It was getting light and the people on the pavements were waking up. Some were rolling up the mats they slept on at night. The street was full of crows hopping around the cow dung. Near the steps at the entrance was a beat-up old taxi, the driver asleep with his face against the side window.

"The Taj Mahal," I said getting in.

III

The only inhabitants of Bombay who take no notice of the "right of admission" regulations in force at the Taj Mahal are the crows. They drop slowly onto the terrace of the Inter-Continental, laze on the Mogul windows of the older building, perch amid the branches of the mango trees in the garden, and hop on the perfect carpet of lawn that surrounds the swimming pool. They would go and drink from the pool itself or peck at the orange peel in your martini, were it not for a very efficient servant in livery who chases them off with a cricket bat, as though in some absurd match orchestrated by a whimsical film director. You have to be careful of the crows, they have very dirty beaks. The Bombay town council has had to arrange for the enormous reservoirs that feed the city's aqueduct to be covered over, because more than once the crows, who themselves arrange for the re-introduction into the "life cycle" of the corpses the Parsees lay out on the Towers of Silence (there are quite a number of towers in the Malabar Hill area), have dropped the odd mouthful into the water supply. But even with these measures the town council certainly hasn't resolved the hygiene problem, because then there are the problems of the rats, the insects, the seepage from the sewers. It's as well not to drink the water in Bombay. But you can drink it at the Taj Mahal which has its own purifiers and is proud of its water. Because the Taj is not a hotel: with its eight hundred rooms it is a city within a city.

When I arrived in this city I was received by a doorman dressed as an Indian prince with red sash and turban, who led me as far as the lobby, all done out in brass, where there were other employees likewise disguised as maharajas. Probably they imagined that I too was disguised, though in reverse – that I was a tycoon dressed up as a nobody – and they busily set about finding me a room in the noble wing of the building, the part that has the antique furniture and the view of the Gateway of India. For a moment I was tempted to tell them that I wasn't there for aesthetic purposes, but just to sleep in consciousless comfort, and that they could put me anywhere they liked, in a room with shamefully modern furniture, even the skyscraper of the Inter-Continental was okay by me. But then I thought it would be cruel to disappoint them like this. The Peacock Suite, however, I refused. It was too much for one person on his own; but it wasn't a question of price, I explained, to maintain the kind of style I had opted for.

The room was impressive, my case had come along ahead of me by some mysterious route and stood on a wicker stool, the bath was already full of water and foam. I sank into it and then wrapped myself in a linen towel. The windows opened onto the Arabian Sea. The sun was almost up now, and a pinkish light tinged the beach; beneath the Taj Mahal the life of India had begun to swarm once again. The heavy curtains of green velvet ran sweetly and softly as a theatre curtain; I drew them across the scene and the room was reduced to half-light and silence. The lazy, comforting hum of the big fan lulled me and I just managed to reflect that this too was a superfluous luxury, since the room temperature was perfect, when suddenly I found myself at an old chapel on a Mediterranean hillside. The chapel was white and it was hot. We were hungry and Xavier, laughing, was pulling out some sandwiches and cool wine from a basket. Isabel was laughing too, while Magda stretched out on a blanket on the grass. Far below us was the blue of the sea and a solitary donkey dawdled in the shade of the chapel. But it wasn't a dream, it was a real memory; I was looking into the dark of the room and seeing that distant scene which seemed like a dream because I'd slept for a long time; my watch told me it was four in the afternoon. I stayed in bed quite a while, thinking of those times, going back over landscapes, faces, lives. I remembered the trips in the car along the pinewoods by the sea, the nicknames we gave each other, Xavier's guitar and Magda's shrill voice announcing in mock serious tones, like a fairground showman: "Ladies and gentlemen, your attention please, we have among us The Italian Nightingale!" And I would play along with her and launch into old Neapolitan songs, mimicking the out-dated warbling of singers in the old days, while everybody laughed and applauded. Amongst ourselves, and I was resigned to it, I was "Roux", short for Rouxinol, Portuguese for nightingale. But the way they said it it seemed an attractive, even exotic name, so there was no reason to take offence. And then I went back over the following summers. Magda crying – I thought, why? Was it right perhaps? And Isabel, and her illusions. And when those memories took on an unbearable clarity, sharp as if beamed on the wall by a projector, I got up and left the room.

Six o'clock is a bit too late for lunch and a bit too early for dinner. But at the Taj Mahal, said my guidebook, thanks to its four restaurants, you can eat at any time. The Rendez-Vous was on the top floor of the Apollo Bunder, but it was really too intimate. And too expensive. I dropped into the Apollo Bar and chose a table by the big terrace window looking out on the first lights of the evening; the seafront was a garland. I drank two gin-and-tonics which put me in a good mood and wrote a letter to Isabel. I wrote for a long time, in a constant stream, with passion, and told her everything. I wrote about those distant days, about my trip, and about how feelings flower again with time. I also told her things I would never have thought of telling her, and when I re-read the letter, with the reckless amusement of someone who has drunk on an empty stomach, I realized that really that letter was for Magda, it was to her I'd written it, of course it was, even though I'd begun, "Dear Isabel"; and so I screwed it up and left it in the ashtray, went down to the ground floor, into the Tanjore Restaurant and ordered a slap-up meal, exactly as a prince dressed up as a nobody would have. And then when I'd finished eating it was night-time; the Taj was coming to life and sparkled with lights; on the lawn near the pool the liveried servants stood ready to chase off the crows; I sat myself down on a couch in the middle of that hall, big as a football field, and set about watching luxury. I don't know who it was said that in the pure activity of watching there is always a little sadism. I tried to think who it was, but couldn't, yet I felt that there was some truth in the statement: and so I watched with greater pleasure, with the perfect sensation of being just two eyes watching while I myself was elsewhere, without knowing where. I watched the women and the jewels, the turbans, the fezes, the veils, the trains, the evening dresses, the moslems and the millionaire Americans, the oil magnates and the spotless, silent servants: I listened to laughter, to phrases comprehensible and incomprehensible, whispers, rustlings. And this went on and on the entire night, till dawn almost. Then, when the voices thinned out and the lights were dimmed, I leant my head on the cushions of the couch and fell asleep. Not for long though, because the first boat for Elephanta casts off from right in front of the Taj at seven o'clock; and along with an older Japanese couple, cameras round their necks, I was on that boat.

IV

"What are we doing inside these bodies," said the man who was preparing to stretch out in the bed next to mine.

His voice didn't have an interrogative tone, perhaps it was not a question, just a statement, made in his way; in any case it would have been a question I couldn't have answered. The light that came from the station plat-forms was yellow and traced its thin shadow on the peeling walls, moving lightly across the room, prudently and discreetly I thought, the same way the Indians themselves move. From far away came a slow monoto-nous voice, a prayer perhaps, or a solitary, hopeless lament, the kind of cry that expresses nothing but itself, asks nothing of anyone. I found it impossible to make out any words. India was this too: a universe of flat sounds, undifferentiated, indistinguishable.

"Perhaps we're travelling in them," I said.

Some time must have passed since his first comment, I had lost myself in distant thoughts: a few minutes' sleep maybe. I was very tired.

He said: "What did you say?"

"I was referring to our bodies," I said. "Perhaps they're like suitcases; we carry ourselves around."

Above the door was a blue nightlight, like the ones they have in night trains. Blending with the yellow light that came from the window it gave a pale green, aquarium-like glow. I looked at him and in the greenish, almost funereal light, I saw the profile of a sharp face with a slightly aquiline nose. He had his hands on his chest.

"Do you know Mantegna?" I asked. My question was absurd too, but certainly no less so than his.

"No," he said, "is he Indian?"

"Italian," I said.

"I only know the English," he said, "the only Europeans I know are English."

The distant cry picked up again and with greater intensity; it was really shrill now. For a moment I thought it might be a jackal.

"An animal?" I said, "What do you think?"

"I thought he might be a friend of yours," he replied softly.

"No, no," I said, "I meant the voice coming from outside – Mantegna is a painter, but I never knew him, he's been dead a few hundred years."

The man breathed deeply. He was dressed in white, but he wasn't a Moslem, that much I had understood. "I've been to England," he said, "but I used to speak French too, if you prefer we can speak French." His voice was completely neutral, as if he were making a statement across the counter in a government office; and this, I don't know why, disturbed me. "It's a Jain," he said after a few seconds, "he's lamenting the evil of the world."

I said: "Oh, right," because now I'd realized he was talking about the wailing in the distance.

"There aren't many Jains in Bombay," he said then,

with the tone of someone explaining something to a tourist. "In the south, yes, there are still a lot. As a religion it's very beautiful and very stupid." He said this without any sign of contempt, still speaking in the neutral tone of someone giving evidence.

"What are you?" I asked. "If you'll forgive my indiscretion."

"I'm a Jain," he said.

The station clock struck midnight. The distant wail suddenly stopped, as if the wailer had been waiting for the hour to strike. "Another day has begun," said the man, "from this moment it's another day."

I said nothing, his assertions didn't exactly encourage conversation. A few minutes went by; I had the impression that the platform lights had grown dimmer. My companion's breathing had slowed, with pauses between each breath, as if he were sleeping. When he spoke again I started. "I'm going to Varanasi," he said, "what about yourself?"

"To Madras," I said.

"Madras," he repeated, "oh yes."

"I want to see the place where it's said the Apostle Thomas was martyred; the Portuguese built a church there in the sixteenth century, I don't know what's left of it. And then I have to go to Goa, I'm going to do some work in an old library – that's why I came to India."

"Is it a pilgrimage?" he asked.

I said no. Or rather, yes, but not in the religious sense of the word. If anything, it was a private journey, how could I put it, I was only looking for clues.

"You're a Catholic, I suppose," said my companion.

"All Europeans are Catholics, in a way," I said. "Or Christians anyway, which is practically the same thing."

The man repeated the adverb I'd used as if he were savouring it. His English was very elegant, with little pauses and the conjunctions slightly drawled and hesitant, the way people speak in certain universities I realized. "Practically ... Actually," he said, "what strange words. I heard them so many times in England, you Europeans often use these words." He paused a moment longer than usual, but I was aware that he hadn't finished what he was saying. "I never managed to establish whether out of pessimism or optimism," he went on. "What do you think?"

I asked him if he could explain himself better.

"Oh," he said, "it's difficult to explain more clearly. Yes, sometimes I ask myself if it's a word which indicates arrogance, or whether on the contrary it merely signifies cynicism. And a great deal of fear as well, perhaps. You follow me?"

"I don't know," I said. "It isn't that simple. But perhaps the word 'practically' means practically nothing."

My companion laughed. It was the first time he had laughed. "You are very clever," he said, "you got the better of me and at the same time you proved me right, practically."

I laughed too, and then said at once: "However, in my case it is practically fear."

We fell silent for a while, then my companion asked if he could smoke. He rummaged in a bag he had near the bed and the room filled with the aroma of one of those small, scented Indian cigarettes made from a single leaf of tobacco.

"I read the gospels once," he said. "It's a very strange book."

"Only strange?" I asked.

He hesitated. "Full of arrogance too," he said. "No offence meant you understand."

"I'm afraid I don't quite see what you mean," I said.

"I was referring to Christ," he said.

The station clock struck half-past midnight. I felt sleep getting the better of me. From the park beyond the platforms came the cawing of crows. "Varanasi is Benares," I said. "It's a holy city. Are you going on a pilgrimage too?"

My companion stubbed out his cigarette and coughed lightly. "I'm going there to die," he said, "I have only a few days left to live." He arranged his cushion under his head. "But perhaps it would be wise to sleep," he went on. "We don't have many hours to rest – my train leaves at five."

"Mine leaves just a little later," I said.

"Oh, don't worry," he said, "the attendant will come and wake you up in time. I don't suppose we shall have occasion to see each other again in the form in which we meet today, these present suitcases of ours. I wish you a pleasant journey."

"A pleasant journey to you too," I answered.

V

My guidebook maintained that the best restaurant in Madras was the Mysore Restaurant in the Coromandel, and I was most curious to check it out. In the boutique on the ground floor I bought a white shirt, Indian style, and a pair of smart trousers. I went up to my room and took a long bath to wash away the grime of the journey. The rooms in the Coromandel are furnished in imitation colonial style, but in good taste. My room was at the back of the building and looked out over a yellowish clearing surrounded by wild vegetation. It was a huge room, with two large beds covered with two quite beautiful counterpanes. At the far end, near the window, was a writing table with a central drawer and then three drawers at each side. It was by pure chance that I chose the bottom drawer on the right to put my papers in.

I ended up going down much later than I would have liked, but in any case the Mysore stayed open till midnight. The restaurant had French windows opening onto the swimming pool and small round tables in booths of green-lacquered bamboo. The lights on the tables had blue shades and there was a great deal of atmosphere. A musician on a red-upholstered dais entertained the diners with some very discreet music. The waiter led me through the tables and was most helpful when it came to advising me what to eat. I treated myself to three dishes and drank fresh mango juice. The customers were almost all Indians, but at the table nearest mine were two Englishmen who had a professional look about them and talked about Dravidian art. They kept up a very pretentious, knowledgeable conversation, and for the duration of my meal I amused myself by checking in my guidebook to see if the information they were giving each other was correct. Occasionally one of them got a date wrong, but the other didn't seem to notice. Conversations you overhear by chance are curious: I would have said they were old university colleagues, and only when they agreed not to take tomorrow's flight for Colombo did I realize that they had only met that day. Going out I was tempted to stop in the English Bar in the lobby, but then I reflected that my tiredness had no need of alcoholic assistance and I went up to my room.

When the telephone rang I was cleaning my teeth. For a moment I thought it might be the Theosophical Society, since they had promised they would confirm by phone, but moving to pick it up I rejected that hypothesis, given the time. Then it crossed my mind that before dinner I had mentioned in reception that one of the bathroom taps wasn't working properly. And in fact it was reception. "Excuse me, sir, there's a lady who wishes to speak to you."

"I beg your pardon," I answered with my toothbrush between my teeth.

"There's a lady who wishes to speak to you," the

receptionist repeated. I heard the click of a switch and a low, firm female voice said: "I am the person who had your room before you, I've absolutely got to speak to you. I'm in the lobby."

"If you give me five minutes I'll meet you in the English Bar," I said. "It should still be open."

"I'd prefer to come up myself," she said, without giving me time to reply, "it's a matter of the utmost importance."

When she knocked I had scarcely finished getting dressed again. I told her the door was unlocked and she opened it, stopping a moment in the doorway to look at me. The light in the corridor was dim. All I could see was that she was tall and wore a silk scarf round her shoulders. She came in, closing the door after her. I was sitting on an armchair in the full light and I got up. I didn't say anything, waiting. And in fact it was she who spoke first. She spoke without advancing into the room, in the same low, firm voice she'd had on the telephone. "Please forgive this intrusion. You must think me incredibly rude – unfortunately there are circumstances when one can hardly be otherwise."

"Listen," I said, "India is mysterious by definition, but puzzles are not my forte. Spare me any pointless effort."

She looked at me with a show of surprise. "It's simply that I left some things that belong to me in the room," she said calmly. "I've come to get them."

"I thought you'd be back," I said, "but frankly I didn't expect you so soon, or rather, so late."

The woman watched me with increasing amazement. "What do you mean?" she muttered.

"That you are a thief," I said.

The woman looked toward the window and took the silk scarf from her shoulders. She was beautiful, I thought, unless perhaps it was the light filtered through the lampshade that gave her face a distant, aristocratic look. She wasn't so young any more yet her body was very graceful.

"You are very categoric," she said. She passed a hand across her face, as if wanting to brush away her tiredness, or a thought. Her shoulders trembled in a brief shiver. "What does it mean, to steal?" she asked.

The silence fell between us and I caught the exasperating sound of the dripping tap. "I called before dinner," I said, "and they assured me they'd fix it right away. It's a noise I can't stand; I'm afraid it won't help me to get to sleep."

She smiled. She was leaning on the rattan chest of drawers, an arm hanging down her side as though she were very tired. "I think you'll have to get used to it," she said. "I was here a week and I asked them to fix it dozens of times, then I gave up." She paused a moment. "Are you French?"

"No," I answered.

She looked at me with a defeated air. "I came in a taxi from Madurai," she said. "I've been travelling all day." She wiped her forehead with her silk scarf as if it were a handkerchief. For a moment her face took on what looked like a desperate expression. "India is horrible," she said, "and the roads are hell."

"Madurai is a very long way," I came back. "Why Madurai?"

"I was going to Trivandrum, then from there I would have gone to Colombo."

"But Madras has a flight to Colombo too," I objected.

"I didn't want to take that one," she said. "I had my reasons. It won't be difficult for you to work them out." She made a tired gesture. "Anyhow, I'll have missed it by now."

She gave me a questioning look and I said: "It's all there where you left it in the bottom drawer on the right."

The writing table was behind her; it was made of bamboo with brass corners and had a large mirror above in which I could see the reflection of her naked shoulders. She opened the drawer and took the bundles of documents held together by an elastic band.

"It's too stupid," she said. "One does something like this and then forgets everything in a drawer. I kept it in the hotel safe for a week and then I left it here while I was packing."

She looked at me as if waiting for me to agree.

"Yes, it is pretty stupid," I said. "The transfer of all that money was an operation of high-class fraud, and then you go and make such a dumb mistake."

"Perhaps I was too nervous," she said.

"Or too busy getting revenge," I added. "Your letter was remarkable, a ferocious vendetta, and he can't do anything about it, if you make it in time. It's just a question of time."

Her eyes flickered, looking at me in the mirror. Then she turned suddenly, quivering, her neck tense. "You read my letter as well!" she exclaimed with contempt.

"I even copied part of it out," I said.

She looked at me with amazement, or with fear perhaps. "Copied it," she muttered. "Why?"

"Only the last part," I said, "I'm sorry, I couldn't help it. And anyway, I don't even know who it was to. All I understood was that he's a man who must have made you suffer a great deal."

"He was too rich," she said. "He thought he could buy everything, people included." Then she made a nervous gesture, indicating herself, and I understood.

"Listen, I think I see more or less how it was. You didn't exist for years, you were always just an empty name, until one day you decided to give a reality to the name. And that reality is you. But I know only the name you signed with; it's a very common name and I have no desire to know anything else."

"Right," she said, "the world is full of Margarets."

She moved away from the writing table and went to sit on the stool by the dressing table. She put her elbows on her knees and her face in her hands. She sat a long time like that, without saying anything, hiding her face.

"What do you plan to do?" I asked.

"I don't know," she answered. "I'm very frightened. I must get to that bank in Colombo tomorrow, otherwise all that money's going to go down the drain."

"Listen a moment," I said, "it's late. You can't go to Trivandrum now, and anyway you wouldn't get there in time for the plane tomorrow. Tomorrow morning there's a plane for Colombo from here; you're lucky because if you turn up early you'll get a seat, and according to the register you've already left the hotel."

She looked at me as if she didn't understand. She looked at me a long time, intensely, weighing me up.

"As far as I'm concerned you really have gone," I added, "and there are two comfortable beds in this room."

She seemed to relax. She crossed her legs and sketched a smile. "Why are you doing this?" she asked.

"I don't know," I said. "Perhaps I feel sympathetic toward people on the run. And then, I stole something from you too."

"I left my case at reception," she said.

"Perhaps it would be wise to leave it there and pick it up tomorrow morning. I can lend you some pyjamas: we are almost the same size."

She laughed. "That only leaves the problem of the tap," she said.

I laughed too. "But you're used to it by now, I gather. The problem is all mine."

VI

"Le corps humain pourrait bien n'être qu'une apparence," he said. *"Il cache notre réalité, il s'épaissit sur notre lumière ou sur notre ombre."*

He raised his hand and made a vague gesture. He was wearing a large white tunic and the sleeve rose and fell on his thin wrist. "Oh, but that isn't theosophy. Victor Hugo, *Les Travailleurs de la Mer.*" He smiled and poured me something to drink. He raised his glass full of water as if making a toast.

To what? I thought. And then I lifted my glass too and said: "To light and shadow."

He smiled again. "Please do excuse me for this very frugal meal," he said, "but it was the only way to talk without being too hurried after your brief afternoon visit. I'm sorry that my prior engagements didn't allow me to receive you at greater leisure."

"It's a privilege," I said. "You are very kind, I would never have dared hope so much."

"We rarely receive outside visitors in this centre," he went on in his vaguely apologetic tone. "But from what I gather it seems that you are not simply a curious outsider."

I realized that after my rather mysterious note, my

telephone calls, the afternoon visit in which I had referred only to a "missing person", I could hardly carry on in this cryptic and alarmist way. I would have to explain myself clearly, precisely. But what did I have to ask, after all? Only a remote piece of information, a hypothetical clue: a possible link to bring me closer to Xavier.

"I am looking for someone," I said. "His name is Xavier Janata Pinto, he's been missing almost a year. The last I heard of him he was in Bombay, but I have good reason to believe that he may have been in contact with the Theosophical Society, and that is what brings me here."

"Would it be indiscreet to ask you what reasons you have for believing this?" my host asked.

A waiter came in with a tray and we served ourselves sparingly: I out of politeness, he no doubt out of habit.

"I'd like to know if he was a member of the Theosophical Society," I said.

My host looked at me hard. "He was not," he stated softly.

"But he was corresponding with you," I said.

"He may have been," he said, "but in that case it would be a private correspondence and confidential."

We began to eat vegetable rissoles with some totally tasteless rice. The waiter stood to one side, the tray in his hands. At a nod from my host he quietly disappeared.

"We do have files, but they are reserved for our members. However, these files do not include private correspondence," he explained.

I nodded in silence, because I realized that he was

manipulating the conversation as he chose and it was no good going on with requests that were too direct and explicit.

"Are you familiar with India?" he asked a moment later.

"No," I answered, "this is the first time I've been here. I still haven't really taken in where I am."

"I wasn't referring so much to the geography," he explained. "I meant the culture. What books have you read?"

"Very few," I answered. "At the moment I'm reading one called *A Travel Survival Kit*. It's turning out to be quite useful."

"Very amusing," he said icily. "And nothing else?"

"Well," I said, "a few things, but I don't remember them very well. I must confess to having come unprepared. The only thing I remember fairly well is a book by Schlegel, but not the famous one, his brother I think; it was called: *On the Language and Wisdom of the Indians.*"

He thought a moment and said: "It must be an old book."

"Yes," I said, "published in 1808."

"The Germans were very much attracted by our culture. They have often formulated interesting opinions about India, don't you think?"

"Perhaps," I said, "I'm not in a position to say with any confidence."

"What do you think of Hesse, for example?"

"Hesse was Swiss," I said.

"No, no," my host corrected, "he was German; he only took Swiss citizenship in 1921."

"But he died Swiss," I insisted.

"You haven't told me what you think of him yet," chided my host in a soft voice.

For the first time I sensed a strong feeling of irritation growing inside me. That heavy, dark, close room with its bronze busts along the walls and glass-covered bookcases; that pedantic, presumptuous Indian, manipulating the conversation as he chose; his manner, somewhere between the condescending and the crafty: all this was making me uneasy and that uneasiness was rapidly turning into anger, I could feel it. I had come here for quite other reasons and he had coolly ignored them, indifferent to the urgency which he must have appreciated from my phone calls and my note. And he was subjecting me to idiotic questions about Hermann Hesse. I felt I was being taken for a ride.

"Are you familiar with *rosolio*?" I asked him. "Have you ever tried it?"

"I don't think so," he said, "what is it?"

"It's an Italian liqueur, it's rare now. They drank it in the bourgeois salons of the nineteenth century – a sweet, sticky liqueur. Hermann Hesse makes me think of *rosolio*. When I get back to Italy I'll send you a bottle, if it's still to be found, that is."

He looked at me, uncertain as to whether this was ingenuousness or insolence. Naturally it was insolence: that was not what I thought of Hesse.

"I don't think I'd like it," he said drily. "I don't drink, and what's more I detest sweet things." He folded his napkin and said: "Shall we make ourselves comfortable for tea?"

We moved to the armchairs near the bookcase and the

servant came in with a tray as if he'd been waiting behind the curtain. "Sugar?" my host asked, pouring tea into my cup.

"No, thanks," I answered, "I don't like sweet things either."

There followed a long and embarrassing silence. My host sat with his eyes closed, quite still; for a moment I thought he might have dozed off. I tried to work out his age, without success. He had an old but very smooth face. I noticed that he wore lace-up sandals on bare feet.

"Are you a gnostic?" he asked suddenly, still keeping his eyes closed.

"I don't think so," I said. And then added: "No, I'm not, just a little curious."

He opened his eyes and gave me a sly or ironic look: "And how far has your curiosity taken you?"

"Swedenborg," I said, "Schelling, Annie Besant: something of everybody." He seemed interested and I explained: "I came to some of them in roundabout ways, Annie Besant, for example. She was translated by Fernando Pessoa, a great Portuguese poet. He died in obscurity in 1935."

"Pessoa," he said, "of course."

"You know him?" I asked.

"A little," he said. "The way you know the others."

"Pessoa said he was a gnostic," I said. "He was a Rosicrucian. He wrote a series of esoteric poems called *Passos da Cruz*."

"I've never read them," said my host, "but I know something of his life."

"Do you know what his last words were?"

"No," he said. "What were they?"

"Give me my glasses," I said. "He was very shortsighted and he wanted to enter the other world with his glasses on."

My host smiled and said nothing.

"A few minutes before that he wrote a note in English: he often used English in his personal notes – it was his second language – he had grown up in South Africa. I managed to photocopy that note; the writing was very uncertain of course. Pessoa was in agony, but it is legible. You want me to tell you what it said?"

My host moved his head back and forth, as Indians do when they nod.

"I know not what tomorrow will bring."

"What strange English," he said.

"Right," I said, "what strange English."

My host got up slowly, he gestured to me to stay where I was and crossed the room. "Please excuse me a minute," he said, going out of the door at the other end of the room. "Do make yourself comfortable."

I sat in my armchair and looked at the ceiling. It must have been very late already, but my watch had stopped. The silence was total. I thought I heard the ticking of a clock in another room, but perhaps it was something wooden creaking, or my imagination. The servant came in without saying a word and took away the tray. I began to feel rather uneasy again, and this together with my tiredness generated a sense of discomfort, a kind of suffering almost. Finally my host came back and, before sitting down, handed me a small yellow envelope. I immediately recognized Xavier's handwriting. I opened the envelope and read the following note: *Dear Master and Friend, the circumstances of my life are not such as to permit me to come back and walk along the banks of the Adyar. I have become a night bird and I prefer to think that my destiny wanted it this way. Remember me as you knew me. Your X.* The note was dated: Calangute, Goa, September 23rd.

I looked at my host in amazement. He had sat down and was watching me with what seemed like curiosity. "So he isn't in Bombay any more," I said. "He's in Goa, at the end of September he was in Goa."

He nodded and said nothing. "But why did he go to Goa?" I asked. "If you know something, tell me."

He clasped his hands together over his knees and spoke calmly. "I don't know," he said. "I don't know what your friend's life is really like, I can't help you, I'm sorry. Perhaps the circumstances of that life of his haven't been propitious, or perhaps he himself wanted it that way; one must never know too much about the mere appearances of other people's lives." He smiled coyly and gave me to understand that he had no more to say to me on the matter. "Are you staying on in Madras?"

"No," I said, "I've been here three days, I'm going tonight, I already have a ticket for the long-distance bus."

I thought I saw an expression of disapproval cross his face.

"It's the reason for my trip," I felt I ought to explain. "I'm going to consult some archives in Goa, I have to do some research. I would have gone anyway, even if the person I'm looking for had not been there."

"What have you seen here in our parts?" he asked.

"I've been to Mahabalipuram and Kanchipuram," I said. "I've visited all the temples."

"Did you stay the night there?"

"Yes, in a little government-run hotel, very cheap: it was what I found."

"I know it," he said. And then he asked: "What did you like most?"

"Lots of things, but perhaps the Temple of Kailasantha. There's something distressing and magical about it."

He shook his head. "That's a strange description," he said. Then he quietly got up and murmured: "I think it's late, I still have a great deal of writing to do tonight. Allow me to show you out."

I got up and he led me down the long corridor to the front door. I stopped a moment in the porch and we shook hands. Going out I thanked him briefly. He smiled and said nothing in reply. Then, before closing the door, he said, "Blind science tills vain clods, mad Faith lives the dream of its cult, a new God is only a word. Don't believe or search: all is hidden." I went down the few steps and walked a little way along the gravel drive. Then all of a sudden I understood, and I turned quickly: they were lines from a poem by Pessoa, only he had said them in English, that was why I hadn't immediately recognized them. The poem was called *Christmas*. But the door was already closed and the servant, at the end of the driveway, was waiting to close the gate after me.

VII

The bus crossed an empty plain with just the occasional sleeping village. After a stretch of road through the hills with hairpin bends that the driver had tackled with a nonchalance I felt was excessive, we were now speeding along enormously long straight quiet roads through the silence of the Indian night. I had the impression that we were going through a landscape of palm groves and paddy fields, but the darkness was too deep to be certain and the light of the headlamps only swept quickly across the landscape when the road made a bend or two. According to my calculations we ought to be quite close to Mangalore, if the bus was keeping to the schedule set out in the timetable. In Mangalore I had two alternatives: I could either wait seven hours for the bus to Goa, or stay for a day in a hotel and take the bus the following day.

It was difficult to decide. During the journey I had slept little and badly, and I felt quite tired; but a whole day in Mangalore was not a particularly attractive proposition. Of Mangalore my guidebook said: "Situated on the Arabian Sea, the city preserves practically nothing of its past. It is a modern industrial city, laid out on a straightforward urban grid and with an anonymous look about it. One of the few cities in India where there really is nothing to see."

I was still weighing up the pros and cons when the bus stopped. It couldn't be Mangalore; we were in open country. The driver turned off the engine and a few passengers got out. At first I thought it was a brief stop to give the travellers a chance to relieve themselves, but after about a quarter of an hour I felt that the stop was unusually protracted. What's more, the driver had calmly sunk down against the back of his seat and looked as if he had gone to sleep. I waited another quarter of an hour. The passengers who had stayed on board were sleeping quietly. In front of me an old man with a turban had taken a long strip of material from a basket and was rolling it up with patience, carefully smoothing out the folds at every turn of the cloth. I whispered a question in his ear, but he turned round and looked at me with an empty smile to show he hadn't understood. I looked out of the window and saw that near the edge of the road, in a large sandy clearing, was a sort of dimly lit warehouse. It looked like a garage made of boards. There was a woman at the door. I saw someone go in.

I decided to ask the driver what was going on. I didn't want to wake him, he'd been driving for a long time, but perhaps it was as well to find out. He was a fat man, sleeping with his mouth open; I touched his shoulder and he looked at me confused.

"Why have we stopped?" I asked. "This isn't Mangalore."

He pulled himself up and smoothed his hair. "No sir, it isn't."

"So why have we stopped?"

"This is a bus-stop," he said, "we're waiting for a connection."

The stop wasn't indicated on the timetable on my ticket, but by now I had got used to this kind of Indian surprise. So I asked him about it without any show of being taken aback, out of pure curiosity. It was the bus for Mudabiri and Karkala, I discovered. I made a suggestion that seemed logical to me. "And can't the passengers going to Mudabiri and Karkala wait on their own, without us waiting with them?"

"There are people on that bus who will get on our bus to go to Mangalore," the driver replied calmly. "That's why we're waiting."

He stretched out on the seat again to let me know that he would like to go back to sleep. I spoke to him again in the tone of one who is resigned: "How long will we be here?"

"Eighty-five minutes," he replied, with an exactness that I didn't know whether to interpret as British politeness or a form of refined irony. And then he said: "Anyway, if you're tired of waiting in the bus, you can get out. There's a waiting room at the side here."

I decided it might be wise to stretch my legs a little to make the time pass faster. The night was soft and damp with a strong scent of herbs. I took a turn round the bus, smoked a cigarette leaning on the steps at the back, and then headed for the "waiting room". It was a long low shed with an oil lamp hanging at the door. On the door jamb someone had stuck a picture of a divinity unknown to me, done in coloured chalk. Inside were a dozen or so people, sitting on the benches along the walls. Two women standing by the door were talking busily to each other. The few passengers who had got off the bus were scattered round the circular bench in the middle around a support post to which were attached leaflets of various colours and a yellowing notice that might have been a timetable or a government directive. Sitting on the bench at the far end was a boy of about ten with short trousers and sandals. He had a monkey with him, hanging onto his shoulders, its head hidden in his hair and its little hands clasped together round the neck of its master in an attitude of affection and fear. Apart from the oil lamp on the door, there were two candles on a packing case: the light was very dim and the corners of the shed were in darkness. I stood a few moments looking at these people who appeared to take no notice of me at all. I thought it strange, this boy alone in this place with his monkey, even if it is common to see children alone with animals in India; and immediately I thought of a child who was dear to me, and of his way of cuddling a teddy-bear before going to sleep. Perhaps it was that association that led me toward the boy, and I sat down next to him. He looked at me with two beautiful eyes and smiled, and I smiled back at him; and only then did I realize with a sense of horror that the tiny creature he was carrying on his shoulders was not a monkey but a human being. It was a monster. Some atrocity of nature or terrible disease had shrivelled up his body, distorting shape and size. The limbs were twisted and deformed with no proportion or sense other than that of an appalling grotesque. The face too, which I now glimpsed amid the hair of his carrier, had not escaped the devastation of the disease. The rough skin and wound-like wrinkles gave him that monkeyish look which together with his features had prompted my mistake. The only thing that was still human about that face were the eyes: two very small, sharp, intelligent eyes, which darted uneasily in every direction as if terrified by a great and imminent danger, wild with fear.

The boy said hello in a friendly way. I said good evening to him and found myself unable to get up and go away.

"Where are you going?" I asked him.

"We're going to Mudabiri," he said smiling, "to the temple of Chandranath."

He spoke fairly good English, without hesitations. "Your English is good," I said, "who taught you?"

"I learnt at school," said the boy proudly. "I went for three years." Then he made a gesture, turning his head slightly, his face taking on an expression of apology. "He doesn't understand English, he wasn't able to go to school."

"Of course," I said, "I understand."

The boy stroked the hands clinging together over his chest. "He's my brother," he said affectionately, "he's twenty." Then assuming an expression of pride again, he said: "But he knows the Scriptures, he knows them off by heart, he's very intelligent."

I tried to look casual, as if a little distracted and immersed in my own thoughts, so as to disguise the fact that I lacked the courage to look at the person he was talking about. "What are you going to Mudabiri for?" I asked.

"There are the festivals," he said. "The Jain come

from all over Kerala, there are a lot of pilgrims around now."

"And you are pilgrims too?"

"No," he said, "we do the rounds of the temples, my brother is an Arhant."

"I'm sorry," I said, "but I don't know what that means."

"An Arhant is a Jain prophet," the boy explained patiently. "He reads the *karma* of the pilgrims, we make a lot of money."

"So he's a fortune-teller."

"Yes," said the boy innocently, "he sees the past and the future." Then making a professional association of ideas, he asked me: "Would you like to know your *karma*? It only costs five rupees."

"Okay," I said, "ask your brother about my *karma*."

The boy spoke softly to his brother and the brother replied in a whisper, looking at me with his darting eyes.

"My brother asks if he can touch your forehead," the boy told me. The monster nodded agreement, waiting.

"Sure he can, if it's necessary."

The fortune-teller stretched out his twisted little hand and placed his forefinger on my forehead. He stayed that way a few moments staring at me intently. Then he withdrew his hand and whispered some words in his brother's ear. A short, excited argument followed. The fortune-teller spoke quickly, he seemed annoyed and irritated. When they had finished arguing the boy turned to me with a wounded look.

"So," I asked, "can I hear it?"

"I'm sorry," he said, "my brother says it isn't possible, you are someone else."

"Oh, really," I said, "who am I?"

The boy spoke to his brother again and the brother answered briefly. "It doesn't matter," translated the boy, "that's only *maya*."

"And what is *maya*?"

"It's the outward appearance of the world," the boy replied, "but it's only illusion, what counts is the *atma*." Then he consulted his brother and confirmed with conviction: "What counts is the *atma*."

"And what is the *atma*?"

The boy smiled at my ignorance. "The soul," he said, "the individual soul."

A woman came in and sat on the bench opposite us. She was carrying a basket with a child asleep inside. I looked at her and she made a rapid gesture of bowing her head in her hands as a sign of respect.

"I thought we only had our *karma* inside us," I said, "the sum of our actions, of what we have been and what we shall be."

The boy smiled again and spoke to his brother. The monster looked at me with his small sharp eyes and held up two of his fingers. "Oh, no," explained the boy, "there's your *atma* as well, it's there together with the *karma*, but it's a separate thing."

"Well then, if I'm another person, I'd like to know where my *atma* is, where it is now."

The boy translated for the brother and a rapid exchange followed. "It's difficult to say," he came back to me, "he can't do it."

"Try asking him if ten rupees would help," I said.

The boy told him and the monster stared into my face with his small eyes. Then he spoke a few words directly to me, very quickly. "He says it's not a question of rupees," the boy translated, "you're not there, he can't tell you where you are." He gave me a nice smile and went on: "but if you want to give us the ten rupees, we'll take them anyway."

"Sure I'll give you them," I said, "but at least ask him who I am now."

The boy turned on his indulgent smile again and then said: "but that's only your *maya*, what use is it knowing that?"

"Of course," I said, "you're right, no use at all." Then I had an idea and said: "Ask him to try and guess."

The boy looked at me in astonishment. "To guess what?"

"To guess where my *atma* is," I said. "Didn't you say he had prophetic powers?"

The boy translated my question and the brother gave him a brief answer. "He says he can try," he said, "but he can't guarantee anything."

"It doesn't matter, let him try just the same."

The monster stared at me very intensely, for a long time. Then he made a gesture with his hand and I waited for him to speak, but he didn't. His fingers moved lightly in the air, tracing waves, then he cupped his hands as if to lift some imaginary water. He whispered a few words. "He says you are on a boat," the boy also spoke in a whisper. The monster made a gesture with his palms turned outward and stopped still.

"On a boat," I said. "Ask him where, quickly, what boat?"

The boy put his ear to his brother's whispering mouth. "He sees a lot of lights. He can't see any more than that, it's no good asking him."

The fortune-teller had again assumed his initial position, his face hidden in his brother's hair. I took out ten rupees and handed them over. I went out into the night and lit a cigarette. I stopped to look at the sky and the dark bank of vegetation along the edge of the road. The bus for Mudabiri shouldn't be far away now.

VIII

The custodian was a wrinkly, friendly-faced little old man with a circle of white hair that stood out against his olive skin. He spoke perfect Portuguese and when I told him my name he smiled broadly nodding his head back and forth, apparently very pleased to see me. He explained that the prior was taking vespers and had asked me to please wait for him in the library. He handed me a note which read: *Welcome to Goa. I'll meet you in the library at 18.30. If you need something, you can ask Theotónio. Father Pimentel.*

Theotónio led me up the stairs chattering away. He was a great talker and had no inhibitions; he had lived a long time in Portugal, in Vila do Conde, he said, where he had some relatives; he liked Portuguese cakes, especially *pão de ló*.

The staircase was made of dark wood and led up to a large, dimly lit gallery with a long table and a globe. On the wall were life-size paintings of serious-looking bearded figures, darkened by time. Theotónio left me at the door to the library and hurried back downstairs as if he had a lot to do. The room was large and cool with a strong stale smell. The bookshelves had baroque twirls and ivory inlays, but were in bad condition, I thought.

There were two long central tables with big twisted candlestick legs and some smaller low tables near the walls with church-style pews and old wicker armchairs. I took a look at the first shelf on the right. There were some books on patristics and some seventeenth-century Jesuit chronicles. I took out two books at random and sat down on the armchair near the entrance. On the next table a book lay open, but I didn't look at it; I leafed through one of the books I had taken, the *Relaçao do novo caminho que fez por Terra e por Mar, vindo da India para Portugal, o Padre Manoel Godinho da Companhia de Iesu*. The colophon said: *Em Lisboa, na Officina de Henrique Valente de Oliveira, Impressor del Rey N.S., Anno 1665*. Manoel Godinho had a pragmatic vision of life, which didn't clash in the slightest with his profession as guardian of the Catholic faith in that enclave of counter-reform besieged by the Hindu pantheon. His narrative was exact and circumstantial, free of pomposity or rhetoric. He had no love of metaphors or similes, this priest; he had a strategic eye, dividing the earth into promising and unpromising areas, and he thought of the Christian West as the centre of the world. I had got to the end of a long preface dedicated to the King, when, without knowing, in response to what signal, I had the sensation I was not alone. Perhaps I heard a slight squeak or sigh; or, more likely, I simply had the sensation you get when you're being watched. I raised my eyes and scanned the room. In an armchair between the two windows at the other end of the room, the dark mass, which when I came in I had thought was a cloak carelessly thrown over the back of the chair, turned slowly round, exactly as if he had been waiting for the moment I would look at him, and stared at me. He was an old man with a long hollow face, his head covered by some kind of hat whose shape I couldn't make out.

"Welcome to Goa," he grunted. "You have committed the imprudence of coming from Madras; the road is full of bandits."

He had a very hoarse voice, and made occasional gurgling noises. I looked at him in amazement. It seemed odd to me that he should use the word "bandits", and odder still that he knew where I had come from.

"And the overnight stop in that horrible place certainly won't have been very reassuring for you," he went on. "You are young and enterprising, but you are often afraid; you wouldn't make a good soldier, perhaps cowardice would get the better of you." He looked at me indulgently. I don't know why, but I felt a deep embarrassment which prevented me from replying. But how did he know about my trip, I thought, who had told him?

"Don't worry," said the old man, as if guessing what I was thinking. "I've got plenty of informers, I have."

He pronounced this last remark in an almost menacing tone, and this made a strange impression on me. We were speaking in Portuguese, I remember, and his words were cold and dull, as if a great distance lay between them and his voice. Why did he speak like that, I wondered, who on earth could he be? The long room was in semi-darkness and he was at the other end, quite a distance from me, his body partly hidden by a table. All this, together with the surprise, had prevented me from seeing his face. But now I saw that he wore a triangular hat of soft cloth and had a long grey beard that brushed against his chest which was covered by a corset embroidered with silver thread. His shoulders were wrapped in a roomy black cloak cut in an antique style, with puffed out sleeves. He read the uneasiness on my face, shifted his seat and sprang up toward the middle of the room with an agility I would never have suspected. He was wearing high boots turned down at the thigh and had a sword at his hip. He made a somewhat ridiculous theatrical gesture, tracing a generous spiral with his right arm which he then placed over his heart, exclaiming in a booming voice: "I am Afonso de Albuquerque, Viceroy of the Indies!"

Only then did I realize that he was mad. I realized it and at the same time, in an odd way, I thought that he really was Afonso de Albuquerque, and none of this surprised me: it just made me feel tired and indifferent, as if everything was predestined and unavoidable.

The old man looked me over warily, suspiciously, his small eyes gleaming. He was tall, majestic, arrogant. I realized that he was expecting me to speak; and I spoke. But the words came out of their own accord, involuntarily. "You look like Ivan the Terrible," I said, "or rather the actor who played him."

He said nothing and put his hand to his ear.

"I mean in an old film," I explained, "you made me think of an old film." And while I was saying this, a glow spread across his face, as if a fire were blazing in a hearth nearby. But there was no hearth, the room was getting darker and darker, perhaps it had been the last ray of the setting sun.

"What have you come here for?" he shouted suddenly. "What do you want from us?"

"Nothing," I said, "I don't want anything. I came here to do some archive research, it's my job. This library is almost unknown in the West. I'm looking for old chronicles."

The old man tossed his large cloak over one shoulder, just as theatre actors do when they're about to fight a duel. "It's a lie!" he cried vehemently. "You had a different reason for coming here."

His violence didn't frighten me, I wasn't afraid he would attack me: yet I did feel a strange sense of subjugation, as if he had uncovered some guilt that I had been concealing from him. I lowered my eyes in shame and saw that the book open on the table was Saint Augustine. I read these words: *Quo modo praesciantur futura.* Was it just a coincidence, or did someone want me to read those words? And who, if not the old man? He had told me he had his informers, that was his word, and this I found menacing and inescapable.

"I've come here to search for Xavier," I confessed. "It's true, I'm searching for Xavier."

He looked at me triumphantly. There was irony in his expression now, and scorn perhaps. "And who is Xavier?"

I saw this question as a betrayal, because I felt he was going back on a tacit agreement, that he "knew" who Xavier was and shouldn't have had to ask me. And I didn't want to tell him, I felt that too.

"Xavier is my brother," I lied.

He laughed cruelly and pointed his forefinger at me.

59

"Xavier doesn't exist," he said. "He's nothing but a ghost." He made a gesture that took in the whole room. "We are all dead, haven't you realized that yet? I am dead, and this city is dead, and the battles, the sweat, the blood, the glory and my power, all dead, all utterly in vain."

"No," I said, "there is always something survives."

"What?" he demanded. "His memory? Your memory? These books?"

He took a step toward me and I was swept by a great sense of horror, because I already knew what he was about to do, I don't know how, but I already knew. With his boot he kicked a little bundle that lay at his feet, and I saw it was a dead mouse. He shifted the creature across the floor and grunted with derision: "Or this mouse?" He laughed again and his laughter froze my blood. "I am the Pied Piper of Hamelin!" he cried. Then his voice became friendly, called me professor and said: "I'm sorry if I woke you."

"I'm sorry if I woke you," said Father Pimentel.

He was a man of about fifty with a solid build and a frank manner. He held out his hand and I got up, confused.

"Oh, thank you," I said, "I was having a bad dream."

He sat on the small armchair near mine and made a reassuring gesture. "I got your letter," he said. "The archives are at your disposal, you can stay as long as you like. I imagine you'll be sleeping here this evening, I've prepared a room for you." Theotónio came in with a tray of tea and a cake that looked like *pão de ló*.

"Thank you," I said, "your hospitality is most kind. But I won't be stopping this evening, I'm going on to Calangute, I've hired a car. I want to try and find out something about somebody. I'll be back in a few days' time."

IX

Another thing that can happen to one in the course of a lifetime is to spend a night in the Hotel Zuari. At the time it may not seem a particularly happy adventure; but in the memory, as always with memories, refined of immediate physical sensations, of smells, colour, and the sight of a certain little beasty beneath the washbasin, the experience takes on a vagueness which improves the overall image. Past reality never seems quite as bad as it really was: the memory is a formidable falsifier. Distortions creep in, even when you don't want them to. Hotels like this already populate our fantasy: we have already come across them in the books of Conrad or Somerset Maugham, in the occasional American film based on the novels of Kipling or Bromfield: they seem almost familiar.

I arrived at the Hotel Zuari late in the evening and I had no choice but to stay there, as is often the way in India. Vasco da Gama is a small town in the State of Goa, an exceptionally ugly, dark town with cows wandering about the streets and poor people wearing Western clothes, an inheritance of the Portuguese period; it thus has all the misery without the mystery. Beggars abound, but there are no temples or sacred places here, and the beggars don't beg in the name of Vishnù, nor lavish benedictions and religious formulas on you: they are taciturn and dazed, as if dead.

In the lobby of the Hotel Zuari there is a semi-circular reception desk behind which stands a fat male receptionist who is forever talking on the telephone. He books you in, talking on the telephone; still talking on the telephone he gives you the keys; and at dawn, when the first light tells you you can finally dispense with the hospitality of your room, you will find him talking on the telephone in a monotonous, low, indecipherable voice. Who is the receptionist of the Hotel Zuari talking to?

There is also a vast dining room on the first floor of the Hotel Zuari, so as not to contradict the sign on the door; but that evening it was dark and there were no tables and I ate on the patio, a little courtyard with bougainvillaea and heavily scented flowers and low little tables with small wooden benches, all dimly lit. I ate scampi as big as lobsters and a mango dessert, I drank tea and a kind of wine that tasted of cinnamon; all for a price equivalent to three thousand lira, which cheered me up. Along one side of the patio ran the veranda onto which the rooms looked out; a white rabbit was hopping over the stones of the courtyard. An Indian family was eating at a table at the far end. At the table next to mine was a blonde woman of indefinable age and faded beauty. She ate with three fingers, the way the Indians do, making perfect little balls of rice and dipping them in the sauce. She looked English to me, and so, as it turned out, she was. She had a mad glint in her eyes, but only every now and then. Later she told me a story that I don't really think I should put down here. It may well have been an anxiety dream. But then the Hotel Zuari is not a place for happy dreams.

X

"I worked as a mailman in Philadelphia, at eighteen already walking the streets with my bag over my shoulder, without fail, every morning, in summer when the tar turns to molasses and in winter when you slip on the icy snow. For ten years, carrying letters. You don't know how many letters I've carried, thousands and thousands. They were all upper class, rich, the people on the envelopes. Letters from all over the world: Miami, Paris, London, Caracas. Good morning, sir. Good morning, madam. I'm your mailman."

He raised an arm and pointed to the group of young people on the beach. The sun was going down and the water sparkled. Near us some fishermen were preparing a boat. They were half naked, wearing loincloths. "Here we're all equal," he said, "there's no upper class, no ladies and gentlemen." He looked at me and a sly expression crossed his face. "Are you a gentleman?"

"What do you think?"

He looked at me doubtfully. "I'll answer that later." Then he pointed to the huts made of palm leaves on our left that leant against the dunes. "We live there, it's our village, it's called Sun Village." He pulled out a little wooden box with papers and a mixture and rolled himself a cigarette. "Smoke?"

"Not as a rule," I said, "but I'll have one now if you're offering."

He rolled another for me and said: "It's good this mixture, it makes you feel happy. Are you happy?"

"Listen," I said, "I was enjoying your story, go on with it."

"Well," he said, "one day I was walking down a street in Philadelphia, it was very cold, I was delivering the mail, it was morning, the city was covered in snow, Philadelphia is so ugly. I was walking down these huge roads, then I turned into a smaller street, long and dark, with just a blade of sunlight that had managed to break through the smog lighting the end of the street. I knew that street, I delivered there every day, it was a street that ended in the wall of a car repair place. Well, you know what I saw that day? Try and guess."

"I've no idea," I said.

"Try and guess."

"I give up, it's too difficult."

"The sea," he said. "I saw the sea. At the end of the street there was a beautiful blue sea with the waves crested with foam and a sandy beach and palm trees. How about that, eh?"

"Strange," I said.

"I'd only seen the sea at the cinema before, or on postcards from Miami or Havana. And this was exactly like those, an ocean, but with nobody there, the beach deserted. I thought, they've brought the sea to Philadelphia. And then I thought, I'm seeing a mirage, like you read about in books. What would you have thought?"

"The same," I said.

"Right. But the sea can't get to Philadelphia. And mirages happen in the desert when the sun is burning down and you're desperately thirsty. And that day it was freezing cold with the city full of dirty snow. So I crept up, very slowly, drawn on by that sea and feeling like I'd like to dive right in, even if it was cold, because the blue was so inviting and the waves were gleaming, lit by the sun." He paused a moment and took a drag on his cigarette. He smiled with an absent, distant expression, reliving that day. "It was a picture. They'd painted the sea, those bastards. They do it sometimes in Philadelphia, it's an idea the architects had, they paint on the concrete, landscapes, valleys, woods and the rest, so that you don't feel so much like you're living in a shithole of a city. I was about a foot away from that sea on the wall, with my bag on my shoulder; at the end of the street the wind made a little eddy and beneath the golden sand there was litter and dry leaves whirling around, and a plastic bag. Dirty beach, in Philadelphia. I looked at it a moment and thought, if the sea won't go to Tommy, Tommy will go to the sea. How about that?"

"I was familiar with another version," I said, "but the concept is the same."

He laughed. "You've got it," he said. "And so you know what I did? Try and guess."

"I've no idea."

"Try and guess."

"I give up," I said, "it's too difficult."

"I took the lid off a trashcan and dumped in my mailbag. You wait there, letters. Then I made a dash back to the head office and asked to speak to the boss. I need three months' salary in advance, I said, my father has a serious illness, he's in hospital, look at these doctor's certificates. He said: first sign this statement. I signed it and took the money."

"But was your father really ill?"

"Sure he was, he had cancer. But he was going to die just the same, even if I did go on carrying the mail to the ladies and gents of Philadelphia."

"That's logical," I said.

"I brought just one thing away with me," he said. "Try and guess what."

"Really, it's too difficult, it's no good, I give up."

"The telephone directory," he said with satisfaction.

"The telephone directory?"

"Right, the Philadelphia telephone directory. That was my only luggage, it's all that's left me of America."

"Why?" I asked. I was getting interested.

"I write postcards. It's me who writes the ladies and gents of Philadelphia now. Postcards with a nice sea and the deserted Calangute beach, and on the back I write: Best wishes from mailman Tommy. I've got up to letter C. Obviously I skip the areas I'm not interested in and send them without a stamp, the person who gets it pays."

"How long have you been here?" I asked him.

"Four years," he said.

"The Philadelphia phone directory must be long."

"Yep," he said, "it's enormous. But then, I'm not in any hurry, I've got my whole life."

The group on the beach had lit a large fire, someone began to sing. Four people left the group and came towards us, they had flowers in their hair and smiled at us. A young woman was holding a girl of about ten by the hand.

"The party's about to begin," said Tommy. "It'll be a big party, it's the equinox."

"Equinox nothing," I said, "the equinox is the twenty-third of September, it's December now."

"Well, something like that anyway," answered Tommy. The girl kissed him on the forehead and then went off again to the others.

"They're not that young any more though, are they?" I said. "They look like middle-aged parents."

"They're the ones who came here first," Tommy said, "the Pilgrims." Then he looked at me and said: "Why, what are you like?"

"Like them," I said.

"You see," he said. He rolled himself another cigarette, split it in two and gave me half. "What are you doing round here?" he asked.

"I'm looking for someone called Xavier, he may have passed through here from time to time."

Tommy shook his head. "But is he happy for you to be looking for him?"

"I don't know."

"So don't look for him then."

I tried to give him a detailed description of Xavier. "When he smiles he looks sad," I finished.

A girl left the group and called to us. Tommy called back to her and she came towards us. "My girlfriend," Tommy explained. She was a pale blonde girl with vacant eyes and two childish pigtails gathered up on her head. She swayed as she walked, a little hesitant. Tommy asked her if she knew a guy who looked like this and this, repeating my description. She smiled incongruously and didn't answer. Then she sweetly stretched out her hands to us and whispered: "Hotel Mandovi."

"The party's beginning," said Tommy. "Come along."

We were sitting on the edge of a very primitive boat with a crude float like a catamaran's. "Maybe I'll come over later," I said. "I'm going to lie down a while in the boat and take a nap." As they were going away I couldn't resist it and shouted after him that he had forgotten to tell me if I was a gentleman like the rest. Tommy stopped, raised his arms and said: "Try and guess."

"I give up," I shouted, "it's too difficult." I got out my guidebook and lit matches. I found it almost at once. They described it as a, "popular, top range hotel," with a respectable restaurant. In Panaji, once Nova Goa, inland. I stretched out on the bottom of the boat and looked at the sky. The night was truly magnificent. I followed the constellations and thought about the stars and the time when we used to study them and the afternoons spent at the planetarium. All at once I remembered how I had learnt them, classifying them by the intensity of their light: Sirius, Canopus, Centaurus, Vega, Capella, Arcturus, Orion . . . And then I thought of the variable stars and the book of a person dear to me. And then of the dead stars, whose light still reaches us, and of the neutron stars in the last stage of evolution, and the feeble ray they emit. In a low voice I said: pulsar. And almost as if reawakened by my whisper, or as if I had started a tape recorder, I heard the nasal phlegmatic voice of Professor Stini saying: When the mass of a dying star is greater than double the solar mass, the matter is no longer in a state such as to arrest the process of concentration which then proceeds ad infinitum; no radiation will ever leave that star again and it is thus transformed into a black hole.

XI

How odd life is. The Hotel Mandovi takes its name
from the river it stands beside. The Mandovi is a wide,
calm river with a long estuary lined with beaches,
almost like sea beaches. On the left there is the port of
Panaji, a river port for small steamers pulling barges
laden with merchandise. There are two dilapidated
gangways and a rusty jetty. And when I arrived, right by
the edge of the jetty, as if it were coming out of the river,
the moon rose. It had a yellow halo and was full and
blood-coloured. I thought, red moon, and instinctively I
started whistling an old song. The idea came like a short
circuit. I thought of a name, Roux, and then
immediately of those words of Xavier's: "I have become
a night bird"; and then everything seemed so obvious,
stupid even, and I thought: Why didn't I think of it
before?

I went into the hotel and took a look around. The
Mandovi was built in the late fifties and already has an
air of being old. Perhaps it was built when the
Portuguese were still in Goa. I don't know what it was,
but the place seemed to have preserved something of the
fascist taste of the period. Perhaps it was the big lobby
that looked like a station waiting room, or perhaps it

was the impersonal, depressing post-office or civil-service-style furniture. Behind the desk were two employees; one had a striped tunic, and the other a slightly shabby black jacket and an air of importance about him. I went to the latter and showed him my passport.

"I'd like a room."

He consulted the register and nodded.

"With terrace and river view," I specified.

"Yes, sir," he said.

"Are you the manager?" I asked as he was filling out my form.

"No, sir," he answered. "The manager is away, but I am at your service for anything you may need."

"I'm looking for Mr. Nightingale," I said.

"Mr. Nightingale isn't here any more," he said perfectly naturally. "He left some time ago."

"Do you know where he went?" I asked, trying to keep sounding natural myself.

"Normally he goes to Bangkok," he said. "Mr Nightingale travels a lot, he's a businessman."

"Oh, I know," I said, "but I thought he might have come back."

The man raised his eyes from the form and looked at me with a puzzled expression. "I couldn't say, sir," he said politely.

"I thought there might be someone in the hotel in a position to give me some more precise information. I'm looking for him for an important piece of business. I've come from Europe specially." I saw he was confused and took advantage of it. I took out a twenty-dollar bill and slipped it under the passport. "Business deals cost money," I said. "It's annoying to come a long way for nothing, if you see what I mean."

He took the note and gave me back my passport. "Mr. Nightingale comes here very rarely these days," he said. He assumed an apologetic expression. "You'll appreciate," he added, "ours is a good hotel, but it can't compete with the luxury hotels." Perhaps it was only at that moment that he realized he was saying too much. And he also realized that I appreciated his saying too much. It happened in a glance, an instant.

"I have to clinch an urgent deal with Mr. Nightingale," I said, though with the clear impression that this tap had now been turned off. And it had. "I am not concerned with Mr. Nightingale's business affairs," he said politely but firmly. Then he went on in a professional tone: "How many days will you be staying, sir?"

"Just tonight," I said.

As he was giving me the key I asked him what time the restaurant opened. He replied promptly that it opened at eight-thirty and that I could order from the menu or go to the buffet which would be laid on in the middle of the room. "The buffet is Indian food only," he explained. I thanked him and took the key. When I was already at the lift I turned back and asked innocuously, "I imagine Mr. Nightingale ate in the hotel when he was staying here." He looked at me without really understanding. "Of course," he replied proudly. "Our restaurant is one of the finest in the city."

Wine costs a lot in India, it is almost all imported from Europe. To drink wine, even in a good restaurant, confers a certain prestige. My guidebook said the same thing: to order wine means to bring in the head waiter. I gambled on the wine.

The head waiter was a plump man with dark rings round his eyes and Brylcreemed hair. His pronunciation of French wines was disastrous, but he did all he could to explain the qualities of each brand. I had the impression he was improvising a little, but I let it go. I made him wait a good while, studying the list. I knew I was breaking the bank, but this would be the last money I spent to this end: I took a twenty-dollar bill, laid it inside the list, closed it and handed it to him. "It's a difficult choice," I said. "Bring me the wine Mr. Nightingale would choose."

He showed no surprise. He strutted off and came back with a bottle of Rosé de Provence. He uncorked it carefully and poured a little for me to try. I tasted it but didn't give an opinion. He didn't say anything either, impassive. I decided that the moment had come to play my card. I drank another sip and said: "Mr. Nightingale buys only the best, I've heard, what do you think?"

He looked at the bottle with inexpressive eyes. "I don't know, sir, it depends on your tastes," he replied calmly.

"The fact is that my tastes are very demanding too," I said. "I only buy the best." I paused to give more emphasis to what I was saying, and at the same time to make it sound more confidential. I felt as though I were in a film, and I was almost enjoying the game. The sadness would come later, I knew that. "Very refined," I finally said, stressing "refined", "and in substantial quantities, not just a drop at a time."

He looked at my glass again without expression and went on with the game. "I gather that the wine is not to your liking, sir."

I was sorry that he had upped the stakes. My finances were running low, but at this point it was worth getting to the bottom of the business. And then I was sure that Father Pimentel would be able to make me a loan. So I accepted his raise and said: "Bring me back the list, please, I'll see if I can choose something better."

He opened the list on the table and I slipped in another twenty dollars. Then I pointed to a wine at random and said: "Do you think Mr. Nightingale would like this?"

"I'm sure he would," he replied attentively.

"I'd be interested to ask him personally," I said. "What would you advise?"

"If I were in sir's position I would look for a good hotel on the coast," he said.

"There are a lot of hotels on the coast, it's difficult to find just the right one."

"There are only two really good ones," he answered. "You can't go wrong: Fort Aguada Beach and the Oberoi. They are both magnificently located with charming beaches, and palm trees that go right down to the sea. I'm sure you will find both to your liking."

I got up and went to the buffet. There were a dozen trays on a spirit-warmer. I took some food at random, picking here and there. I stopped by the open window, my plate in my hand. The moon was already nice and high and reflected in the river. Now the melancholy was setting in, as I had foreseen. I realized I wasn't hungry. I crossed the room and went to the door. As I was going out, the head waiter made a slight bow. "Could you have the wine brought up to my room," I said. "I'd prefer to drink it on the terrace."

XII

"Excuse the banality of the remark, but I have the impression we've met before," I said. I lifted my glass and touched it against hers on the bar. The girl laughed and said: "I have the same impression myself. You look strangely like the man I shared a taxi with this morning from Panaji."

I laughed too. "Oh well, it's no good denying it, I'm the very man."

"You know that sharing that cab was an excellent idea?" she added with an air of practicality. "The guidebooks say the taxis are very cheap in India, but it's not true, they'd take the shirt off your back."

"Let me recommend a reliable guidebook some time," I said with authority. "Our taxi went outside the city, hence the price trebles. I had hired a car, but I had to give it up because it was too expensive. In any case, the major advantage for me was to be able to make the trip in such pleasant company."

"Stop," she said, "don't take advantage of the tropical night and this hotel amongst the palms. I'm susceptible to compliments and I would let myself be chatted up without offering any resistance. It wouldn't be fair on your part." She lifted her glass too and we laughed again.

The description of magnificence given by the head waiter of the Mandovi erred only by default. The Oberoi was more than magnificent. It was a white, crescent-shaped building which exactly followed the curve of the beach along which it was built, a bay protected by a promontory to the north and cliffs to the south. The main lounge was a huge open space that continued out onto the terrace, from which it was separated only by the bar where drinks were served on both sides. On the terrace, tables had been laid for dinner, decorated with flowers and lamps. Hidden away somewhere in the dark a piano was softly playing Western music. Actually, thinking about it, the whole effect was too much in the line of luxury tourism, but at the time this didn't bother me. The first diners were taking their places at the tables on the terrace. I told the waiter to reserve us a corner table in a discreet position and a little away from the light. Then I suggested another aperitif.

"As long as it's not alcoholic," the girl said and then went on in her playful tone: "I think you're going a bit fast, what makes you assume I'll accept your offer of dinner?"

"To tell the truth I had no intention of offering dinner," I confessed candidly. "I've almost run out of what few reserves I had and each of us will have to pay our own way. We'll simply be dining at the same table; we're alone, we can keep each other company, it seemed logical to me."

She said nothing and just drank the fruit-juice the waiter had served her. "And then it's not true we don't know each other," I went on, "we got to know each other this morning."

77

"We haven't even introduced ourselves," she objected.

"It's an omission that's easily enough remedied," I said. "I'm called Roux."

"And I'm called Christine," she said. And then added: "It's not an Italian name, is it?"

"What difference does it make?"

"Actually, none," she admitted. And then sighed: "Your technique is truly irresistible."

I confessed that I had no intention of trying any technique or of chatting her up at all, that I had started off with the idea of a lively dinner with a friendly conversation between equals. Something like that anyway. She looked at me with a mock imploring look, and still with the same playful tone protested: "Oh no, do chat me up, please, sweet talk me, do, say nice things to me, I'm terribly in need of that sort of thing." I asked her where she'd come from. She looked at the sea and said: "From Calcutta. I made a brief stop-over in Pondicherry for a stupid feature on my compatriots who are still living there, but I worked for a month in Calcutta."

"What were you doing in Calcutta?"

"Photographing wretchedness," Christine replied.

"What do you mean?"

"Misery," she said, "degradation, horror, call it what you like."

"Why did you do that?"

"It's my job," she said. "They pay me for it." She made a gesture that perhaps was meant to indicate resignation to her life's profession, and then she asked me: "Have you ever been to Calcutta?"

I shook my head. "Don't go," said Christine, "don't ever make that mistake."

"I imagined that a person like yourself would think that one ought to see as much as possible in life."

"No," she said with conviction, "one ought to see as little as possible."

The waiter signed to us that our table was ready and led us to the terrace. It was a good corner table as I had asked, near the shrubs round the edge, away from the light. I asked Christine if I could sit on her left, so as to be able to see the other tables. The waiter was attentive and most discreet, as waiters are in hotels like the Oberoi. Did we want Indian cuisine or a barbecue? He didn't want to influence us, of course, but the Calangute fishermen had brought baskets of lobsters today, they were all there at the bottom of the terrace ready to be cooked, where you could see the cook in his white hat and the shimmer of glowing coals in the open air. Taking advantage of his suggestion, I ran an eye along the terrace, the tables, the diners. The light was fairly uncertain, there were candles on every table, but the people were distinguishable, with a little concentration.

"I've told you what I do," said Christine, "so what do you do? If you feel like telling me."

"Well, let's suppose I'm writing a book, for example."

"What kind of book?"

"A book."

"A novel?" asked Christine with a sly look.

"Something like that."

"So you're a novelist," she said with a certain logic.

"Oh no," I said, "it's just an experiment, my job is something else, I look for dead mice."

"Come again?"

"I was joking," I said. "I scour through old archives, I hunt for old chronicles, things time has swallowed up. It's my job, I call it dead mice."

Christine looked at me with tolerance, and perhaps with a touch of disappointment. The waiter came promptly and brought us some dishes full of sauces. He asked us if we'd like wine and we said yes. The lobster arrived steaming, just the shell singed, the meat spread with melted butter. The sauces were very heavily spiced, it only took a drop to set your mouth on fire. But then the flames died out at once and the palate filled with exquisite, unusual aromas: I recognized juniper, but the other spices I didn't know. We carefully spread the sauces on our lobster and raised our glasses. Christine confessed that she already felt a bit drunk, perhaps I did too, but I wasn't aware of it.

"Tell me about your novel, come on," she said. "I'm intrigued, don't keep me in suspense."

"But it's not a novel," I protested, "it's a bit here and a bit there, there's not even a real story, just fragments of a story. And then I'm not writing it, I said *let's suppose* that I'm writing it."

Clearly we were both terribly hungry. The lobster shell was already empty and the waiter appeared promptly. We ordered some other things, whatever he wanted to bring. Light things, we specified, and he nodded knowingly.

"A few years ago I published a book of photographs," said Christine. "It was a single sequence on a roll, impeccably printed, just the way I like, with the perforations along the edges of the roll showing, no captions, just photos. It opened with a photograph that I feel is the most successful of my career, I'll send you a copy sometime if you give me your address. It was a blow-up of a detail; the photo showed a young negro, just his head and shoulders, a sports singlet with a sales slogan, an athletic body, an expression of great effort on his face, his arms raised as if in victory; obviously he's breasting the tape, in the hundred metres for example." She looked at me with a slightly mysterious air, waiting for me to speak.

"And so?" I asked. "Where's the mystery?"

"The second photograph," she said. "That was the whole photograph. On the left there's a policeman dressed like a Martian, a plexiglass helmet over his face, high boots, a rifle tucked into his shoulder, his eyes fierce under his fierce visor. He's shooting at the negro. And the negro is running away with his arms up, but he is already dead: a second after I clicked the shutter he was already dead." She didn't say anything else and went on eating.

"Tell me the rest," I said, "you may as well finish the story now."

"My book was called *South Africa* and it had just one caption under the first photograph that I've described, the blow-up. The caption said: *Méfiez-vous des morceaux choisis.*" She grimmaced a moment and went on: "No selections, please. Tell me what your book is about, I want to know the concept behind it."

I tried to think. How could my book turn out? It's difficult to explain the concept behind a book. Christine was watching me, implacable, she was a stubborn girl. "For example, in the book I would be someone who has lost his way in India," I said quickly, "that's the concept."

"Oh no," said Christine, "that's not enough, you can't get off so lightly, there must be more to it than that."

"The central idea is that in this book I am someone who has lost his way in India," I repeated. "Let's put it like that. There is someone else who is looking for me, but I have no intention of letting him find me. I saw him arrive and I have followed him day by day, we could say. I know his likes and his dislikes, his enthusiasms and his hesitations, his generosity and his fears. I keep him more or less under control. He, on the contrary, knows almost nothing about me. He has a few vague clues: a letter, a few witnesses, confused or reticent, a note that doesn't say much at all: signs, fragments which he laboriously tries to piece together."

"But who are you?" asked Christine. "In the book I mean."

"That's never revealed," I answered. "I am someone who doesn't want to be found, so it's not part of the game to say who."

"And the person looking for you who you seem to know so well," Christine asked again, "does he know you?"

"Once he knew me, let's suppose that we were great friends, once. But this was a long time ago, outside the frame of the book."

"And why is he looking for you with such determination?"

"Who knows?" I said. "It's hard to tell, I don't even know that and I'm writing the book. Perhaps he's looking for a past, an answer to something. Perhaps he would like to grasp something that escaped him in the past. In a way he is looking for himself. I mean, it's as if he were looking for himself, looking for me: that often happens in books, it's literature." I paused, as if I had reached a crucial point and said confidentally: "Actually, as it turns out, there are also two women."

"Ah, finally," Christine exclaimed, "now it's getting more interesting."

"I'm afraid not," I went on, "since they too are outside the frame, they don't belong to the story."

"Oh, come on," said Christine, "is everything outside the frame in this book? Why don't you tell me what's inside the frame?"

"I told you, there is someone looking for someone else, there is someone looking for me, the book is his looking for me."

"So then tell me the story a bit better!"

"All right," I said, "it begins like this: he arrives in Bombay, he has the address of a third-rate hotel where I once stayed and he sets off on his search. And there he meets a girl who knew me in the past and she tells him that I've fallen ill, that I went to hospital, and then that I had contacts with some people in the south of India. So he goes off to look for me in hospital, which turns out to be a false trail, and then he leaves Bombay and begins a journey, still with the excuse that he is looking for me, whereas the truth is that he is travelling on his own account for his own reasons; the book is mainly that: his travelling. He has a whole series of encounters, naturally, because when one travels one meets people. He arrives in Madras, goes around the city, the temples in the vicinity, and in a scholarly society he finds a few equivocal clues as to my whereabouts. And in the end he arrives in Goa, where, however, he had to go anyway for reasons of his own."

Christine was following me with attention now, sucking a mint stick and watching me. "In Goa," she said, "Goa of all places, interesting. And what happens there?"

"In Goa there are a lot of other encounters," I continued, "he wanders about here and there, and then one evening he arrives in a certain town and there he understands everything."

"Which is what?"

"Oh, well," I said, "that he wasn't finding me partly for the very simple reason that I had assumed another name. And he manages to find out what it is. In the end it wasn't impossible to find out because it was a name that had to do with himself, in the past. Except that I had altered the name, camouflaged it. I don't know how he got to it, but the fact is that he did, maybe it was luck."

"And what is this name?"

"Nightingale," I said.

"Nice name," said Christine. "Go on."

"Well, then obviously he manages to find out where I am, pretending he has some important business with me: someone tells him that I am in a luxury hotel on the coast, a place like this."

"All righty," said Christine, "now you'd better tell the story really well: we're on set."

"Right," I said, "you've got it: I'll take this as the set. Let's suppose that it's an evening like this evening, warm and spicy, a first-class hotel, by the sea, a big terrace with tables and candles, soft music, waiters who move about attentively, discreetly, the best food, naturally, with an international cuisine. I am sitting at a table with a beautiful woman, a girl like yourself, with a foreign look to her; we are at a table on the opposite side to the one we're sitting at now, the girl facing the sea, while I on the other hand am looking toward the other tables. We are talking amicably, the woman laughs from time to time, you can see from her shoulders, exactly like yourself. At a certain point . . ." I stopped talking and looked across the terrace, my eye running over the people eating at the other tables. Christine had snapped her mint stick, she was holding it in a corner of her mouth as if it were a cigarette, following intently. "At a certain point?" she asked. "What happens at a certain point?"

"At a certain point I see him. He's at a table toward the back on the other side of the terrace. He's sitting the same way I'm sitting, we are face to face. He's with a woman, too, but she has her back to me and I can't see who she is. Perhaps I know her, or I think I know her, she reminds me of somebody, of two people even, she could be either of them. But from a distance like this, with the light from the candles, it's difficult to say for sure, and then the terrace is very big, just like this one. He probably tells the woman not to turn round, he looks at me for a long time, without moving, he has a satisfied expression, he's almost smiling. Perhaps he too thinks he recognizes the woman I'm with, she reminds him of someone, two people even, she could be either of them."

"In short, the man who was looking for you has managed to find you," said Christine.

"Not exactly," I said, "it's not quite like that. He has been looking at me for a long time, and now that he has found me he no longer has any desire to find me. I'm sorry to split hairs but that's how it is. And I have no desire to be found either. We both think exactly the same thing; we look at each other, but nothing more."

"And then?" asked Christine, "what happens next?"

"One of the two finishes drinking his coffee, folds his napkin, adjusts his tie, let's suppose he has a tie, gestures to the waiter to come, pays his bill, gets up, politely draws back the chair of the lady who's with him and who gets up together with him, and goes. That's it, the book is finished."

Christine looked at me doubtfully. "It seems rather a lame ending to me," she says, putting down her cup.

"Right, it does to me too," I said, likewise putting down my cup, "but I can't think of any other solution."

"End of story, end of meal," said Christine. "Both at the same time."

We lit cigarettes and I made a sign to the waiter. "Listen, Christine," I said, "you'll have to excuse me but I've changed my mind, I'd like to buy you dinner, I think I have enough money."

"No way," she protested, "the agreement was explicit, a friendly dinner and we both pay our own."

"Please," I insisted, "take it as an apology for having bored you so much."

"But I've enjoyed myself immensely," retorted Christine, "I insist on going halves."

The waiter came up to me and whispered something she couldn't hear, then padded off in his discreet way. "It's no good arguing," I said, "the dinner is gratis, a customer at the hotel who wishes to remain anonymous has paid for you." She looked at me in amazement. "Must be an admirer of yours," I said, "somebody more gallant than myself."

"Don't talk nonsense," said Christine. Then, pretending to take offence: "It's not fair," she said, "you'd already arranged everything with the waiter."

The verandas that led to the rooms had a roof of polished wood, forming a kind of cloister that looked out on the dark of the vegetation at the back of the hotel. We must have been amongst the first to retire, almost all the other guests had stayed on, in deckchairs, listening to music on the terrace. We walked side by side, in silence. At the end of the veranda a big moth whirred for a moment.

"There's something not quite right in your book," said Christine. "I don't know what exactly, but for me it's not quite right."

"I feel the same way," I answered.

"Listen," said Christine, "you always agree with my criticisms, I can't stand it."

"But I really do agree," I told her, "honestly. It must be a bit like that photograph of yours, the blow-up falsifies the context: you have to see things from a distance. *Méfiez-vous des morceaux choisis.*"

"How long are you staying?" she asked me.

"I'm leaving tomorrow."

"So soon?"

"My dead mice are waiting for me," I said. "To each his own work." I tried to imitate that gesture of resignation she had made when talking about her work. "They pay me for it, like you."

She smiled and fitted the key in the door.